JON AGEE

MR. PUTNEY'S QUACKING DOG

MICHAEL DI CAPUA BOOKS • SCHOLASTIC

This is Mr. Putney.

He has all sorts of unusual friends.

Can you guess what their names are?

Who wakes Mr. Putney up in the morning?

AN ALARMADILLO

Who does Mr. Putney like to jump through?

AN ANTELOOP

Which friend of Mr. Putney's has cold feet?

A SOCKTOPUS

Who does Mr. Putney use to see how tall his nephew is?

A GORULER

Who keeps the rain out of
Mr. Putney's tool shed?

A GIROOF

Who is snooping on Mr. Putney?

A SPYENA

What do you call Mr. Putney's messy lunch companion?

A SLOBSTER

Who is building Mr. Putney's hot tub?

A BOA CONSTRUCTOR

What do you call Mr. Putney's
private locomotive?

A TRAINDEER

Who is Mr. Putney trying to put on a diet?

AN ORANGUTON

Which friend of Mr. Putney's looks just like a pastry?

Who drives Mr. Putney
crazy in the middle of
the afternoon?

A CLANGAROO

Which friend of Mr. Putney's has chicken pox?

A HIPPOSPOTAMUS

Who fits into Mr. Putney's backpack?

A CRAMEL

What do you call Mr. Putney's quacking dog?

A DUCKSHUND

Who does Mr. Putney have a hard time seeing?

AN ELEFAINT

Who is knitting Mr. Putney a sweater?

A WOOLRUS

What does Mr. Putney have on his floor?

A FRUG

Who is always stealing Mr. Putney's ice cream?

A CROOKADILE

Who keeps watch over
Mr. Putney's house?

So now you know
all the names of
Mr. Putney's friends!